Melissa Iwai

Soup Day

SQUARE
FISH

Henry Holt and Company • New York

Henry Holt and Company, LLC, *Publishers since 1866*
Henry Holt® is a registered trademark of Henry Holt and Company, LLC.
Paperback published by Square Fish, an imprint of
Macmillan Publishing Group, LLC
120 Broadway, New York, NY 10271 • mackids.com

Square Fish and the Square Fish logo are trademarks of Macmillan and are
used by Henry Holt and Company under license from Macmillan.

Our books may be purchased in bulk for promotional, educational,
or business use. Please contact your local bookseller or the Macmillan
Corporate and Premium Sales Department at (800) 221-7945 ext. 5442 or
by email at MacmillanSpecialMarkets@macmillan.com.

The Library of Congress has cataloged the hardcover edition as follows:
Iwai, Melissa.   Soup day / by Melissa Iwai. — 1st ed. p. cm.
"Christy Ottaviano Books."

Summary: A mother and child spend a snowy day together buying and
preparing vegetables, assembling ingredients, and playing while their big
pot of soup bubbles on the stove.

Includes a recipe for "Snowy Day Vegetable Soup."
ISBN 978-0-8050-9004-8
[1. Soups—Fiction. 2. Cookery—Vegetables—Fiction. 3. Mother and
child—Fiction.] I. Title.
PZ7.I9528Sou 2010   [E]—dc22   2009029314

Originally published in the United States by Christy Ottaviano Books/
Henry Holt and Company
First Square Fish edition, 2023
Book designed by Elynn Cohen
Acrylics, collage, Adobe Photoshop, and Adobe Illustrator were used to
create the illustrations for this book.
Square Fish logo designed by Filomena Tuosto
Printed in China by RR Donnelley Asia Printing Solutions Ltd., Dongguan
City, Guangdong Province

ISBN 978-0-8050-9004-8 (hardcover)
20 19 18 17 16 15 14 13 12 11
ISBN 978-1-250-88185-4 (paperback)
10 9 8 7 6 5 4 3 2 1

AR: 2.0 / LEXILE: AD44OL

For Jamie and Denis,
my favorite soup eaters

Today is soup day.

I help Mommy pick out the vegetables. She says it's important to choose the freshest ones with the brightest colors.

This is what we put in our basket:

One bunch of
crispy green celery.

Two shiny
yellow onions.

Three long orange carrots.

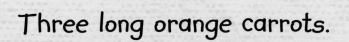

Four smooth tan potatoes.

Five tiny dark green zucchini.

Six big white mushrooms.

Ooops! We almost
forgot the parsley.

Back at home, we wash the vegetables. Then Mommy chops everything into different shapes.

The celery and onions become tiny squares.

The carrots become circles.

The potatoes become cubes.

The parsley becomes confetti.

I get to cut the mushrooms and zucchini
with a plastic knife because they are soft.
Mommy helps my hand.

We pour oil into the big soup pot, and Mommy cooks the onions, celery, and carrots together. This makes them soft.

They sizzle in the oil.

Then we fill the big pot with broth. "Ssssssss!" It makes a loud sound.

I help put in the rest of the vegetables. Mommy covers the pot, and we wait.

For a while we make a city.

We read to each other.

Then we have to escape from a big monster.

Before long, our home
smells like yummy soup.

Mommy checks the pot. We hear the soup bubbling inside. She tastes it. "It needs a little something," she says. Mommy adds some spices.

Now I get to choose which kind
of pasta to add to the soup.

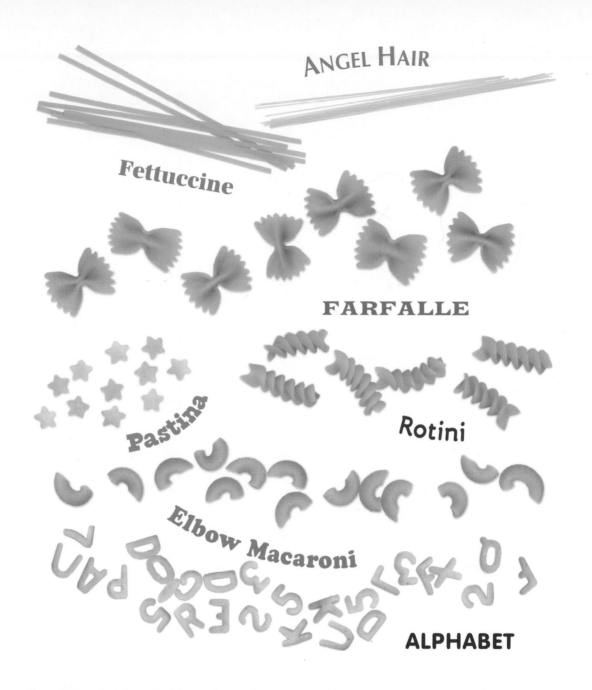

ANGEL HAIR

Fettuccine

FARFALLE

Pastina

Rotini

Elbow Macaroni

ALPHABET

I pick alphabet because I like to eat the letters.
Sometimes they make words.

While we wait for the noodles to cook, we clean up our city.

We return the books to the bookshelf.

We put the monster to sleep.

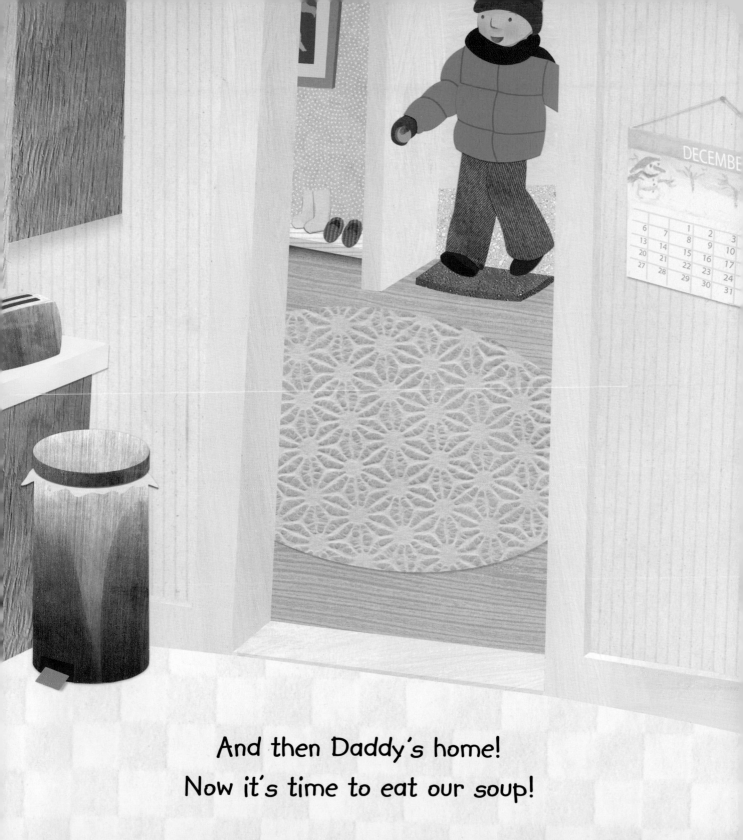

And then Daddy's home!
Now it's time to eat our soup!

Mommy lets me sprinkle the confetti parsley on top. It looks like green snow.

Mmmm!
I love soup day.

Snowy Day Vegetable Soup

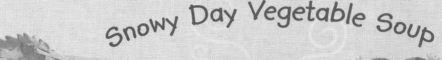

(Makes 6 servings)

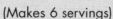
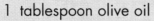

1 tablespoon olive oil
1 cup diced onion
½ cup diced carrots
½ cup diced celery
kosher salt
6 cups chicken, vegetable, or beef stock
2 cups peeled and cubed potatoes

½ cup carrots, sliced into rounds
2 cups zucchini, sliced into rounds
1 cup sliced mushrooms
½ teaspoon freshly ground pepper
1 teaspoon dried thyme
3 ounces dried pasta of choice
¼ cup packed chopped parsley leaves

1. Heat oil in a heavy-bottomed stockpot over medium high heat. When oil is hot, add diced onions, carrots, celery, and a pinch of salt to pot. Sauté until onions are soft and translucent.

2. Add stock. Increase heat to high and bring to a simmer. Once simmering, add potatoes, carrot rounds, zucchini, and mushrooms to pot. Add pepper, thyme, and salt to taste. Reduce heat to low; cover and cook until vegetables are fork tender, about 15 to 20 minutes.

3. Bring water to boil in a medium sauce pan. Add a pinch of salt to water. When water comes to a boil, add pasta and cook to al dente doneness according to package instructions. Drain and add to vegetable soup just before serving.

4. Season to taste with salt and pepper and garnish soup with chopped parsley.
Enjoy!

Note: Please take care to keep children at a distance from burners on the stove.